This book belongs to

_____

Disney's
Winnie the Pooh's Honey Adventures

A READ-ALOUD STORYBOOK COLLECTION

MOUSE WORKS

Find us at www.DisneyBooks.com for more Mouse Works fun!

Pooh's Honey Tree, adapted from the story by Isabel Gaines.
Illustrated by Nancy Stevenson.

Pooh's Honey Hums, adapted from the poems by Don Ferguson.
Illustrated by Bill Langley and Diana Wakeman.

Lots and Lots of Honeypots, adapted from the story by Isabel Gaines.
Illustrated by Josie Lee.

The Big Honeypot Rescue, adapted from the story by Teddy Slater.
Illustrated by Bill Langley and Diana Wakeman.

Better Than Honey, produced by Joshua Morris Publishing, Inc.

Contents

Pooh's Honey Tree

Winnie the Pooh was a bear of little brain. But he had a big, loving heart. And a big, round tummy. Pooh's tummy always looked quite full. But it was always quite hungry. Hungry for honey!

"Oh, bother!" said Pooh, looking in his honeypot. "There's nothing left but the sticky part."
Just then, Pooh heard a buzzing sound.
BUZZ! BUZZ! BUZZ!

Something small and fuzzy flew past his ear.
BUZZ! BUZZ! BUZZ!
"Oh!" said Pooh. "A bee!"
Now, it is true that Pooh was not very
smart. But one thing he knew: where there are
bees, there is honey! So . . .

Pooh followed the bee deep into the
Hundred-Acre Wood.

Soon they came to a tall, tall tree.
A honey tree!

Up the tree Pooh went.

Up.

Up.

Up.

Then, CRACK! A branch broke.
Down the tree Pooh fell.
Down.
Down.
Down.
Pooh rubbed his sore head. All that
head-rubbing made Pooh think. And the first
thing he thought of was Christopher Robin.

13

Pooh picked himself up and set off to find his friend.

When Pooh got to Christopher Robin's house, he saw that his friend had a big blue balloon. "May I borrow your balloon?" Pooh asked.

"Here, Pooh," said Christopher Robin, giving him the balloon.

"Thank you," said Pooh, "I'm going to use this balloon to float up to a honey tree."

"Silly old bear," said Christopher Robin. "The bees will see you. They will not let you near their honey."

At that, Pooh sat down in the mud and rolled around.

"Look!" said Pooh. "The bees will think I'm a little black rain cloud. They will not even know I am there."

"Oh," said Christopher Robin. He sat down under the tree to see what would happen next.

Pooh held on to the balloon. Then he floated all the way up to the top of the honey tree.

Pooh reached into the bees' nest and pulled out a pawful of golden honey.

BUZZ! BUZZ! BUZZ! The bees did not think that Pooh was a little black rain cloud. They thought he was a hungry bear!

Suddenly, the balloon string came undone, and the air swooshed out!

Pooh and his balloon sailed over the treetops.

Finally the balloon lost all its air. Down it came. And down came Pooh.

Pooh landed right in Christopher Robin's arms!

Pooh looked up at the bees in the tree. Then he looked at Christopher Robin. "Oh dear!" Pooh said. "I guess it all comes from liking honey so much!"

Pooh's Honey Hums

When Pooh goes for a float
in his big umbrella boat,
you can bet he's not forgot
his overflowing honeypot.

"My favorite snack,"
says Winnie the Pooh,
"is one jar of honey . . .
or possibly two!"

When Pooh is found high in a tree,
talking to an angry bee,
he isn't trying to be funny.
He's climbed up there to look for honey!

Lots and Lots of Honeypots

One day Pooh saw his little friend Piglet pulling a big wagon.

"What's in your wagon?" asked Pooh.

"Things from my house," said Piglet. "I'm giving them to Christopher Robin."

Tigger bounced up, pulling his wagon. "Christopher Robin will give the things that we don't need to somebody who does need them," he explained.

"Do you have anything that you don't need anymore?" Piglet asked Pooh.

"Let me think," said Pooh, thinking very hard. But he couldn't think of a thing.

Along came Christopher Robin. "I see Piglet's and Tigger's wagons," he said. "Are you going to add anything, Pooh?"

Pooh decided to check his house to see if he had anything to give.

Pooh checked all around his house, but he didn't find a thing. Then he checked his cupboard, and found . . .

"Twenty honey-pots!" exclaimed Christopher Robin, Tigger, and Piglet at the same time.

"Only ten honeypots have any honey in them," said Christopher Robin. "Why do you need so many pots?"

"So I'm all ready if I find some especially yummy honey," smiled Pooh.

"All honey tastes especially yummy to you," Christopher Robin reminded Pooh gently. "Ten pots are enough to store your yummy honey."

"Hmm . . ." said Pooh. He wasn't sure he wanted to share his honeypots.

"Think of everyone who could enjoy some honey if you shared your pots," said Piglet.

"Then they would all be as happy as I am!" agreed Pooh. Pooh decided to give away ten of his pots. His cupboard was nearly empty, but his heart felt full.

37

The Big Honeypot Rescue

One dark night, Pooh heard a strange sound. It wasn't a rumble. It wasn't a grumble. It was a *"Rrrrrr!"*

Pooh got out of his bed. And being a bear of very little brain, he decided to invite the new sound in. "Hello?" he called, flinging open the door.

Suddenly a big, bouncy creature bounded in and knocked Pooh flat on his back!

"*Rrrrr!* Hello," the creature said. "Tigger's my name. T-I—double Guh—Er."

"I'm Pooh," said Pooh.

"What's a Pooh?" asked Tigger.

"You're sitting on one," Pooh informed him.

At that, Tigger jumped up and began to bounce all around Pooh's house!

"Bouncing is what Tiggers do best!" Tigger cried. "But it does make us hungry. Why, it's ricky-diculus how slim-ful I'm getting."

"You're not hungry for honey, I hope," said Pooh, glancing at his honeypot.

"Honey!" Tigger exclaimed, grabbing the honeypot. "That's what Tiggers like best."

"I was afraid of that," said Pooh.

But when Tigger put the honey in his mouth, he yelled, "YUCK!" and bounced right out the door.

Pooh did not know what to expect next! So he decided to sleep right next to his honeypots.

When Pooh woke up, he found himself surrounded by water! It was raining in the Hundred-Acre Wood, and the river had flooded.

At Piglet's house, the water had crept right up into his bed!

Poor Piglet grabbed paper and pen and wrote: "HELP! P . . . P . . . PIGLET. (ME.)" He placed the message in a bottle and threw it into the river.

Meanwhile Pooh was trying to save his honeypots. But as he carried one up to a high branch, he tripped. *Plop!* Pooh got stuck in a honeypot and fell into the river.

No matter how much it rained, the river would never reach Christopher Robin's house. So that is where the Hundred-Acre friends went—even their newest friend, Tigger.

Then Roo made an important discovery. He found Piglet's note.

Christopher Robin told Owl to fly over the water and tell Piglet that his friends were coming to the rescue. Owl quickly found his friends.

But he forgot to tell them about the rescue! Instead, he started to tell a story. "It concerns a distant cousin of mine . . ."

"Look!" cried Piglet. "It's a flutterfall, a falatterfall, a very big w-waterfall!" *Whoosh!* Pooh and Piglet were swept over the edge of the waterfall.

Luckily Pooh floated to the river's edge where Christopher Robin was waiting. Then Piglet popped up, safe and sound in Pooh's honeypot.

Christopher Robin exclaimed, "Pooh, you rescued Piglet with your honeypot!"

"I did?" said Pooh.

"You are a hero, Pooh," declared Christopher Robin. "As soon as the flood is over, I'm going to have a hero party for you."

And that's just what they did.

Better Than Honey

"Today Piglet's coming to visit!" sang Pooh, making up a new song.

But Piglet surprised his friend Pooh Bear — he'd brought their friend Eeyore along!

"Oh dear," Pooh said, setting the table
— three dishes, three spoons, and three cups. "I sure
hope I have enough honey." And then his friend
Tigger showed up!

Pooh took a quick peek in his cupboard to see
how much honey was there.

His tumbly was really quite rumbly, and there
was so little to share!

Just then, he heard someone else knocking,
and in walked friends Rabbit and Owl!
Pooh got two more stools from the corner,
and wiped two more bowls with a towel.

Then Pooh spooned out all of his honey, making sure to share every ounce. He was glad all his friends had come over, 'cause it's sharing the friendship that counts!